What Reggie Did On the Weekend

Seriously!

Lee. M. Winter

D1465341

Copyright © 2016 Lee. M. Winter

All rights reserved.

ISBN: 1533666954
ISBN-13: 978-1533666956

CONTENTS

How I Accidently Ate Cabbage

On the weekend, I accidently ate cabbage.

It all started when Ma plonked a steaming, slimy pile of it on my dinner plate.

I looked at it. I looked at Ma. Ma looked at me.

I said, "What do you expect me to do with this?"

She said, "Eat it."

I said, "But you know I don't eat cabbage."

She said, "You're old enough now to eat cabbage, Reggie."

I said, "Nobody *ever* in the history of the universe has been old enough to eat cabbage."

She said, "Eat it."

I said, "No."

"Eat it."

"No."

"Eat it."

"No."

"Eat it or you don't get any ice-cream."

"That's fine. I don't even *like* ice-cream."

"Yes, you do."

"No, I don't."

"Yes, you do."

"No, I don't."

"Yes, you do."

"No, I don't."

She was technically correct. I *do* like ice-cream. But I couldn't let her win now. If she won, who knew where it would end. *Brussel sprouts?* Or, heaven forbid, *cauliflower??*

And anyway, my hatred of cabbage far outweighs my love of ice-cream.

I couldn't understand what was going on. We'd always had an agreement about cabbage. She didn't serve it to me and I didn't vomit it back up. It was win-win. It had worked fine until now. Why was she trying to move the goal posts??

She tried again.

"All your brothers eat it," she said. I almost laughed out loud. I have five older brothers.
Jon eats his own boogers,

Ron eats his own fingernails,

Don eats his own dandruff,

Lon eats *other people's* dandruff,

And Con eats snails!" (Okay, that was just once, on a dare, and it was at a French Restaurant, but *still*.)

By now Ma's eyes were starting to look a little crazy and tiny beads of sweat shined on her upper lip. She bent her head to mine and spoke in a cold, quiet voice.

"Eat. It. Or. You. Are. Not. Playing. Minecraft."

The Earth rocked on its axis.

So it was going to be like that, was it?

War.

I looked at the cabbage. It sat there pale, green and limp in a pool of its own stinky cabbage water. It wasn't even hot anymore. It was room temperature cabbage. And if there's one thing more disgusting than hot cabbage it's room temperature cabbage.

I looked at Ma. Ma looked at me.

I said, "That's okay. I don't even like Minecraft."

Ma snapped.

"*EAT IT OR YOU'RE GETTING IT FOR BREAKFAST!*"

"See you at breakfast," I said to the cabbage.

She was bluffing. There was no way she'd serve me cabbage for breakfast.

The next morning she served me cabbage for breakfast.

It had been in the fridge overnight so now it was cold cabbage. And if there's one thing more disgusting than room temperature cabbage it's cold cabbage.

I looked at Ma.

Ma looked at me.

She said, "Eat it."

I said, "No."

"Eat it."

"No."

"Eat it."

"No."

"Eat it."

"No."

"Eat it or you're getting it for lunch."

"See you at lunch," I said to the cabbage.

She was bluffing. There was no way she'd serve it to me again for lunch.

She served me the cabbage again for lunch. She'd reheated it in the microwave. And if there's one thing more disgusting than chilled cabbage it's day old cabbage that's been reheated.

Ma said, "Eat it."

I said, "No."

"Eat it."

"No."

"Eat it."

"No."

"Eat it."

"No."

At dinner the cabbage came out again. Chilled. And if there's one thing...well, you get it. *Disgusting.*

But I hadn't eaten in twenty-four hours. I was so hungry I began to see things that weren't there.

In front of my eyes the cabbage turned into a hotdog. A big, juicy, perfectly heated hotdog, with melted cheese on top.

It sat there in a deliciously soft, fluffy bun—not wholemeal—but white, white as a snow-flake.

"Eat me, Reggie," it said in its husky, hotdoggy voice. "You know you want to."

My mouth watered like mad.

I bent my head to take a bite but luckily one of my brothers came in at that moment and slammed the door. I was jolted back to reality.

The talking hotdog disappeared and the soggy, cooked, room temperature, chilled, reheated, chilled again cabbage sat there. Laughing at me.

Ma lost it and began to beg. "Please, Reggie. Just touch a piece with your tongue. You don't even have to swallow it. Just touch it with your tongue and this will all be over. We'll put it behind us and never speak of it again. Please, Reggie. Pleeeease!"

"See you at breakfast," I said to the cabbage. I went to my room with the sound of Ma sobbing behind me.

That night I was so hungry I had dreams about vegetables that I *do* eat. You know, the one's slightly less disgusting than cabbage.

I dreamed of a bowl of carrots as big as a bathtub. Lightly sautéed in melted butter and sprinkled delicately with chopped parsley. I think it was Italian chopped parsley. Next to the carrots was a mountain of steamed baby peas, lightly minted and as fresh as a field of new spring lambs.

I had a fork the size of a garden rake. I was just about to dig in when Ma woke me, calling "Reggie, come down and have breakfast!"

I slumped down the stairs.

I felt sick.

I was weak with hunger. I didn't think I had it in me to keep this up for much longer. Maybe it was time to give in. Let her win.

As I neared the kitchen a delicious smell floated to my nostrils. At first I thought I was seeing things, well, *smelling* things, again. It smelt like...mmm...could it be...Yes! Yes it was! Still warm, fresh out of the oven, homemade double choc chip muffins!

Ma held out the tray of muffins, smiling at me as though I'd just brought home a report card of all As.

"For you, Reggie, darling," she said. "It's over, sweetheart. You win. I see now that I was wrong."

"Really, Ma?" I dared to hope.

"Yes, honey. Take one, you must be starving," she said.

I took a muffin. I had a bite. It was the most delicious muffin I'd ever tasted. The chocolate was creamy, the muffin perfectly moist. And I was sooooo hungry! I stuffed the rest of the muffin into my mouth and chewed fast.

Then Ma did a strange thing.

She threw back her head and started
to laugh. Not just her regular laugh
but more like a witch's cackle. She
cackled and cackled. It was the most
hideous sound I'd ever heard. I
stopped chewing and watched her.

She put down the tray of muffins.
She started dancing around the room,
her eyes crazy.

"Ahahahahah!" she cried. "I win! I win!
Reggie's eating cabbage! Reggie's
eating cabbage!"

She began running all her words
together. "Ahahahahaha! I stayed up

all night cooking at first I made brownies but the cabbage taste was still there so I started again I chopped it up finer I put it into a cheesecake you know you love cheesecake Reggie but the cheesecake came out still tasting like cabbage so I started again at 4am I blitzed the cabbage until it was individual molecules and I baked the molecules of cabbage into my double choc chip muffins...and ahahahahaha...you can't taste the cabbage Reggie you're eating cabbagae!! I win! I win! I haven't had any sleep but I WIN!! Ahahahahahahah!!"

Dad, Jon, Ron, Don, Lon, and Con all tried to calm her down but nothing worked. She kept cackling and dancing.

When Dad threw a bucket of cold water over her and that *still* didn't work he went to the phone and called someone. Two men in white coats came, put Ma on a stretcher and carried her from the house. She was still cackling as they drove away.

I ate six more muffins. She was right. You really couldn't taste the cabbage.

The Amazing Vomiting Boy

On the weekend I was sick.

I woke up at midnight on Saturday and vomited all over myself. Then I vomited over myself again.

I called out to Ma. She came and put me in clean pajamas. I vomited over them.

Then I vomited over Ma.

While Ma was in the shower, Dad came to help. I vomited over him, too. He told me to go to the kitchen and get a bowl to vomit in. On the way to the kitchen I vomited over the dog and the cat. And the goldfish.

I found a bowl and filled it with vomit. Then I filled another bowl with vomit.

I was going through bowls fast. Ma got out of the shower and told me to get in the car. She was taking me to hospital.

For the whole way there, I stuck my head out the window and vomited. I was like Hansel and Gretel, only instead of breadcrumbs I left a trail of vomit.

At the hospital I was rushed into Emergency. Lots of doctors and nurses stood around and watched me vomit. They said they'd never seen anything like it. They called other doctors to come and watch. Some were Skyped in from New York.

They started calling me The Amazing Vomiting Boy. It was pretty cool. Except, you know, for the whole vomiting thing.

I vomited so much that pretty soon the ER was filled with vomit. When it got up to my knees I made a raft from those stick things they put in your mouth to say 'Ahh' and I sailed out the door on a river of vomit.

I sailed past a TV news crew setting up out the front of the hospital. They'd come to get footage of The Amazing Vomiting Boy. Instead they were washed away by the vomit river.

As I sailed down the road people began screaming to get away. You know, from the vomit.

I realized that this vomiting caper was almost like having a super power.

Maybe I could get people to do what I wanted or threaten to drown them in vomit. I could rule the world! Or, even better, I could steer my raft to McDonalds and demand a year's supply of free cheese burgers or I'd fill the drive-thru with vomit!

Then a terrible thing happened. I stopped vomiting. The vomit river drained away.

I didn't get free cheeseburgers.

Ma bought new bowls.

There's a Fly in My Ice-Cream

On the weekend, a fly got stuck in my ice-cream and I wrote a poem about it.

There's a fly in my ice-cream,
I think that it's dead.
No, hang on a minute,
It's moving its head.

Do flys have heads?
I'm really not sure.
Well, whatever *that* is,
It's moving some more.

There's a fly in my ice-cream,
What should I do?
You won't believe this,
Now it's doing a poo!

It *is so doing* a poo,
Honestly, I swear.
Look at that black thing,
Look – right there!
What do you mean you don't care?

Now it's wiping its butt,
It's got a tiny toilet roll!
OMG, that's so funny,
Seriously, lol!

Okay, I might have made that up,
You know, about the tiny toilet roll.
I'm picking the fly out now,
Oh look, it's left a hole.

Of course I'm going to eat it.
Why? What's wrong with that?
It's just a few fly germs,
Stop looking at me like that.

Mmmm, this is really yummy,
Okay, that was a crunchy bit,
Which is weird for vanilla,
Look out – I'm going to be sick!

The Fart Collection

On the weekend my friend, Jimmy, invited me over to his place to see his fart collection.

I'd never seen a fart collection before so I thought, why not? I didn't even know how a person collected farts, although it wasn't a bad idea. My dad is always saying you should keep everything because you never know when you'll need it again.

Jimmy took me to his bedroom.

Against one wall was a set of shelves. On the shelves were jars. I said to Jimmy, "Where are the farts?"

He said, "You're looking at them. They're in the jars."

Of course! It was genius. Fart into a jar and you get to keep it forever. Why hadn't I thought of it?

I had a closer look at the jars on the first shelf. They were labelled with dates, places, and times. The first one said, January 3rd, Sizzler, 6.52pm.

On the next two shelves the jars were organized according to the food Jimmy had eaten before the fart. One whole shelf was dedicated entirely to baked beans. It looked as though Jimmy also quite liked eggs and onions.

The top shelf was just for Christmas and birthday farts, because Jimmy said people always keep the best stuff on the top shelf. Those jars were decorated with tinsel and ribbon.

All of the jars in the collection were made of clear glass and all looked empty. Which made sense, I mean, you can't see farts. But then how could I be sure Jimmy had actually farted into the jars and wasn't just pulling my leg?

Jimmy looked at me proudly. "What do you think?"

I said, "How do I know they're real?"

He told me to me choose a jar. I picked a 'baked bean' from six months ago. He took the lid off. Yep, he was telling the truth. I asked him to put the lid back on.

His Fries are Longer than Mine

On the weekend Ma took me and my brother, Con, to IKEA to buy a new lamp.

As a special treat we ate lunch in the IKEA café. Con and I both chose the salt and pepper squid and a bowl of fries.

For a brief moment there was panic at the table when it looked as though

Con had been given six pieces of squid and I only had five, but a closer look revealed that one of my squid pieces was twisted with another piece, in a kind of squid hug, making it look like there was only one when there were really two. Phew!

Con said that my squid pieces were bigger than his.

I said, "No, they're not."

Con said, "Yes, they are."

I said, "No, they're not."

Con said, "Then let's swap. You won't mind swapping if they are the same."

I said, "No way."

Con said, "Swap or I'll punch you." He

whispered it, so that Ma wouldn't hear.

Ma said, "I heard that."

I quickly licked all my pieces of squid so Con wouldn't want them.

Then I noticed something shocking.

Con's fries were longer than mine.

I said, "Your fries are longer than mine."

Con looked at his fries then he looked at my fries. "No, they're not," he said.

It was obvious. Con's fries had most definitely been cut from a potato twice as big the potato used to cut my fries. This was unacceptable.

I said, "Ma, Con's fries are longer than mine and that's not fair."

Ma said, "Hurry up and eat them, both of you."

How could she be so calm about this? How did she expect me to eat my fries when they were clearly NOT AS GOOD as Con's fries.

I said loudly, "BUT HIS ARE LONGER!"

Ma didn't care.

Even though Ma didn't care, I wanted to prove that I was right. I went and got one of those little tape-measures that IKEA keep handy. I knew they were really for measuring furniture but I couldn't see why they couldn't also be for measuring fries.

Con and I spent the next ten minutes measuring all of our fries.

Ha! Turned out I was right and Con was wrong. His fries were longer.

I said, "You have to let me have half of your long fries."

Con said, "Sure, but you should know that I licked them all while you were getting the tape-measure."

I ate my short fries.

When I finished, Ma was still drinking her coffee so I became bored. I get bored quickly. It's a slight problem of mine.

I was so bored that I started measuring other stuff.

I took off my shoes and measured my toes to see which was longest. I measured my head. I measured Con's head. I measured Con's eyebrows and earlobes. On the floor was a squashed meatball that someone had dropped and stood on. I measured it.

I measured the distance between my eyes. I measured the length of Con's armpit. I measured my belly button. Con bent over to pick up his fork so I measured his butt.

Ma stood up and I tried to measure

her butt and she said "Try it and I'll tie you up with that tape-measure and leave you here with the squashed meatball."

I thought she was joking so I measured her butt.

She wasn't joking.

The meatball and I are now good friends.

I've named him Bert.

My Plan to Take Over the World

On the weekend I made a plan to take over the world.

Not that I actually want to take over the world right now. I mean, I'm kind of busy at the moment. I have my soccer finals coming up, Minecraft takes up a lot of my time...there's this tree in the backyard that I like to hang upside down in, and, well, let's just say I'm busy.

BUT, you never know when my schedule will free up and I might decide to take over the world. When that happens, it will be good to have a plan.

Hey. what's up?

So, obviously, the first thing I need to do is have some way of making everybody in the world do as I say. A supersonic ray gun should do the trick.

I sat and thought about this for a while and realised I had one major problem. I don't know how to build a supersonic ray gun. Think, Reggie! I said to myself.

Well, okay, if you break it down into parts then a supersonic ray gun will need...ah...rays...and, um, supersonic-ness.

This was going to be harder than I thought. Luckily, I remembered my friend Jimmy and his fart collection.

Instead of making a supersonic ray gun I could team up with Jimmy and together we could make a supersonic fart gun! It was brilliant.

With Jimmy's collection we would have an almost endless supply of farts so that part was taken care of. There was still the problem of supersonic-ness, and you know, actually getting the farts into the gun, but we could work out the details later.

Of course, Jimmy would need to understand that *I* was in charge. *I* would be ruling the world and he was along just to supply the farts. It's important to be clear about these things.

So once we have the supersonic fart gun and everybody in the world is doing what I tell them, it will be time to make some changes. Here's my list of changes (it's only a rough draft at this stage):

Make cabbage illegal (anyone caught growing, cooking, or eating cabbage will be sent straight to prison).

Make ice-cream free (*duh!*)

Make it the law that bread must be baked without crusts.

Ban school. (This could be going too far. I might decide that school can be taught on Wednesdays. Wednesday *mornings*. I'll think about it.)

Make the 25th of *every* month Christmas Day (or just Lots of Presents for Kids Day if you don't do Christmas).

Make it the law that parents have to take kids to Disneyland at least twice a year, (more if they want to).

Order all the scientists to work out why you can't tickle yourself and what the purpose of snot is.

Make showering optional. For me. If I decide that *you* stink, then *you* must shower.

Change dinner time around so that dessert has to be eaten first.

Ban all lumps from yoghurt.

Actually, ban lumps from everything. Lumps are unnecessary. Nothing was ever made better with lumps.

Ban the word 'lump'.

That's all I've got so far.

Superhero Names

On the weekend I made up some cool sounding superhero names. Just in case I ever need one.

I have to say, it was quite difficult because, you know, it's important to get just the right tone. Here they are:

Farty McFart Pants

Stinky McFarter

Captain Fart-a-lot

The Fartinator

The Vominator

The Snotinator (he has a gun called the Booger Blaster)

Captain Poop-a-lot

Captain Booger Butt

The Terrible Day at the Beach

On the weekend Ma took us to the beach. I thought it was going to be a fun day.

It wasn't.

Here's what went wrong:
1. I couldn't find my new board-shorts so had to wear an old pair

with Big Bird on the front and Cookie Monster on the back.

2. The old shorts are tight and made me walk like I'd pooped my pants.

3. To punish me for looking like I'd pooped my pants, Don buried me in sand up to my neck. Lon sat on me and bounced a beach ball on my head.

4. The ice-cream van came, but by the time I'd dug myself out of the sand it had sold out of chocolate.

And strawberry.

And vanilla.

And butterscotch.

And cookies and cream.

And crazy mint surprise.

And rainbow delight.

And rainbow disappointment.

They'd run out of everything except bananas. I don't mean banana ice-cream, I mean actual bananas. They were in a bowl on the ledge of the window where the driver stands.

I asked the driver why an ice-cream van would sell bananas and he said he wanted to offer a healthy alternative. I bought a banana.

5. I'd only eaten half my banana when a demented seagull attacked me. I think it wanted the banana. I dropped it in the sand and ran away screaming.

6. To forget about the banana I went for a swim. I was dumped by a huge wave and swallowed about a bucket of seawater.

7. The seawater didn't mix well with the banana and I puked up a mess so disgusting that even the seagull wouldn't touch it.

8. I backed away from the puke mess carefully and stepped in dog poo.

9. While I was scraping the dog poo from my foot, the ice-cream van came back with more ice-cream but drove away again before I could get there.

10. A went for another swim and was chased by a shark (okay, it might have been a dolphin...or seaweed).

11. When I came from the water I had a big lump of sand down my shorts. Now I walked like I'd pooped my pants *and* had the lump to prove it.

12. The crazy seagull that hated me came back with some pals and chased me and my lumpy pants all the way to the car.

Lumpy pants

Getting Rid of My Monster

On the weekend I got rid of the monster under my bed.

His name is Kevin.

Don't ask me how I know his name is Kevin, I just do.

Kevin has lived under my bed forever and ever.

When I was little I was totally freaked out by Kevin. When Ma kissed me goodnight and left the room I would lie there, eyes wide open, listening for Kevin.

Kevin was sneaky. He would be quiet and pretend not to be there but I knew that he was. Don't ask me how I knew, I just did.

Ma would say that if I was scared then I should just look under the bed and then I'd see that there was no monster.

I'm not stupid. I know better than to look under my bed. Everyone knows that monsters under beds are just

waiting for you to look because that's when they grab you.

Eventually I'd get so tired I would fall asleep and that is when Kevin would come out. He'd stand at the end of my bed, in his big, hairy, monster body and stare at me.

I knew this even though I was asleep.

Don't ask me how I knew, I just did.

Anyway, my friend Jimmy came over on Saturday and we were mucking about in my room, and my new awesome handball, with Darthvader on it, rolled under the bed.

I told Jimmy I'd get it later. Of course, you and I know what the problem was, don't we? That's right. Kevin.

The thing is, I really love that ball and really wanted it back. It was time to face Kevin.

After Jimmy went home, I sucked up all my courage. I stood in my room and called out, "Kevin, come out. We need to talk."

Nothing happened. He was pretending he wasn't there.

I said, "Give it up, Kevin. We both know you're there. Get your big, fuzzy body out here."

A heard a sigh and then Kevin came out from under the bed.

We stood looking at each other.

I said, "You're shorter than I imagined." It was true, he was only about as tall as me.

Kevin shrugged his shaggy shoulders and said, "You've got more freckles than I thought. It's hard to see at night when I normally look at you."

I said, "Kevin, you've had it pretty good under my bed but now it's time for you to go. I'm too old to have a monster under my bed."
Kevin shrugged again and said, "Fair enough. Just let me pack my stuff."

He pulled out a red back pack and in it he put two comic books, a teddy bear, and a toothbrush.

"Well, goodbye, Reggie," he said, and then he climbed out the window.
I waved and said, "Good bye, Kevin."

When he was gone I punched the air
and jumped up and down on my bed.
I'd gotten rid of my monster! Woot!

I crawled under the bed and got my
ball. This was the best day ever.

That night, I couldn't sleep.

I missed Kevin.

Some Poems

On the weekend I wrote some poems.

There once was a lady named Rose,
Who was always picking her nose.
She pulled out a booger,
And rolled it sugar,
Then wiped it right onto her clothes.

I know this kid who likes curry,
He's really quite a nut.
He went too far with the chilli one
night,
And blasted a hole in his butt. (*Yeah, I know. He already had a hole in his butt, but this is just a stupid poem, so leave me alone.*)

I threw up in Dad's shoe,
It really wasn't my fault,
My friend, Luke, made me eat worms,
And then he did the bolt.

Dad's shoe was the nearest thing I
could grab,
I really hate that Luke,
You should have heard Dad scream
and shout,
When he stuck his foot in my puke.

The Man Who Wasn't Very Nice

On the weekend I wrote a story about a man who wasn't very nice.

The reason he wasn't very nice was because he hated everything. You can't hate everything *and* still be nice.

Before he became a man who hated everything he was a child who hated everything. (He was probably a baby who hated everything but since babies can't talk it's hard to be sure, although he did cry a lot, if that's anything to go by.)

Anyway, once he was old enough to talk he told his parents that he hated everything. He hated his bedroom, he hated his swing set, he hated his trampoline, and he hated his bike.

His parents tried to help. They asked him why he hated his bike. He said it was because it was blue. So his parents bought him a red one.

He hated it.

No matter what his parents did he still hated everything.

Even though he hated them, the boy ate all his vegetables (including cabbage) and grew into a man; a man who hated everything.

He got a job as a plumber and hated it.

He tried being a postman and hated that, too.

He thought he might not hate a more exciting job so he tried being:

An acrobat

A train driver

A firefighter

A dolphin trainer

A motorcycle stunt rider

He hated them all (okay, he didn't totally hate being a motorcycle stunt rider, he just disliked it very much.)

Eventually, he decided to stay in his house where there were fewer things to hate.

This was okay for a while but then some noisy neighbours moved in. Guess what?

He hated them.

In fact, he hated everyone he ever met, so he packed his things and moved far way to a house on a cliff by the seaside where there were hardly any other people to hate.

Every day he sat on the cliff, watching the ocean and trying not to hate it.

A little girl lived nearby and saw the man sitting by himself every day. She thought he must be lonely and felt sorry for him so she decided to make him a special present.

She planted a geranium seed in a pot and watered it and loved it every day for six weeks. As the geranium plant grew, she spoke to it in a kind voice. She told it all about the lonely man who sat everyday on the cliff.

When the geranium plant grew a beautiful pink flower, the girl carefully wrapped the pot in soft pink tissue paper. She carried it up to the cliff-top and, smiling shyly, gave it to the man.

He hated it and threw it off the cliff.

The girl ran home, crying.

THE END.

(Well, what did you expect? I told you at the start that he wasn't very nice.)

I Like to Poop at Home

On the weekend I went to my friend Jack's house to play and everything was fine until suddenly I needed to use the bathroom.

To do number 2s.

So I had to go home. Yes, that's right. I have to poop at home. While I was at home pooping I made up a poem in my head about it. Here it is:

I like to do my poops at home,

Where I know the toilet is clean.

Please don't ask me to poop in yours,

I don't know where you've been.

It's nothing personal, you understand,

You know I like you a lot.

I'm sure your toilet's fine, in fact,

It's just this thing I've got.

You know I can't poop at school,

Or at Granny and Pop's.

I can never quite relax enough,

To ever hear those plops.

Day trips can be a nightmare,

And don't start me on school camps,

But I can hold it in for days if I have to,

Even with terrible cramps.

The Baby and the Goat

On the weekend I looked after a baby. I didn't do a very good job and the baby was eaten by a goat.

Okay, not quite. This is what happened.

The baby belonged to Ma's friend, Mrs Whitman. Mrs Whitman and the baby came to our house to visit.

I wanted to play outside so Mrs Whitman said the baby could stay outside with me while she had coffee inside with Ma.

I climbed up a tree. The baby sat in its carriage and watched me.

I climbed down the tree. The baby sat in its carriage and watched me.

I rode my bike up and down the path. The baby sat in its carriage and watched me.

I asked the baby what it wanted to do now but it didn't answer. It just sat in its carriage and watched me.

I sang the baby a song and it sat in its carriage and started to scream loudly.

The baby wouldn't stop screaming loudly, even when I stopped singing.

I didn't know what to do so I put a bucket over my head.

The baby stopped screaming.

I took the bucket off my head. I looked at the carriage. The baby was NOT sitting in the carriage watching me. The baby was *GONE.*

I looked under all the bushes, and up the tree, but I couldn't find the baby.

I'd lost the baby.

Losing a baby is bad.

I panicked.

I ran inside and took a potato from the kitchen. From under my bed I scooped up lots of fluff and dust bunnies and stuck them to the top of the potato with my glue stick. I drew a face on the potato.

I ran outside and put the potato-baby in the carriage. Maybe Mrs Whitman wouldn't notice that it wasn't her baby.

I found a stick. I put the bucket back on my head and banged it with the stick to see what it sounded like from inside the bucket.

While I had the bucket on my head, next door's goat came through the fence and ate the potato-baby.

While I was inside getting another potato, I saw Mrs Whitman holding the baby. The real baby, not the potato. She must have come outside and taken the baby when it was screaming and I didn't see her because of the bucket over my head.

So everything turned out okay, but not for the potato-baby, of course. And the goat. It didn't like the fluff and dust bunnies and puked it all up.

My Friend Cheswick

On the weekend I made friends with a piece of cheese.

I know that sounds weird, but hear me out.

It all began when Ma gave me a glass of milk and a piece of cheese as a snack.

The cheese looked funny. It had holes in it. Ma said it was Swiss cheese.

I didn't care what country it came from, it looked funny and I didn't want to eat it.

My brother, Lon, said he would eat it if I didn't want it. (Lon will eat *anything*.)

Then, I noticed that my piece of cheese was talking.

"Hi, Reggie" said the cheese, "My name is Cheswick."

I might have made that up. Cheese can't talk, but I'm certain that's what it was thinking.

So Cheswick and I became friends. Best friends. He was my new BF, which meant I didn't have to eat him because it's not polite to eat your friends.

Cheswick is an awesome friend because he does everything that I do.

Over the weekend we watched TV together.

We played Minecraft together, and we got beaten up by Jon, together.

He even came to my soccer game and cheered for me.

Cheswick and I had so much fun that I couldn't remember what I ever did without him.

On Sunday night, as I tucked Cheswick into bed beside me, Ma said that he was starting to smell bad.

I said that was a mean thing to say about my best friend.

I love Cheswick.

Getting Rid of Cheswick

On the weekend I had to get rid of a rotten, stinky piece of cheese that had been following me around all week.

I threw it in the trash, but I could still smell it.

I took it to the rubbish bin outside, but I could still smell it.

I dug a hole in the backyard and buried it, but I could still smell it.

I dug it up again, wrapped it in ten pieces of tin foil, put it inside an old shoe-box, wrapped the shoe-box in another ten pieces of tin foil, walked to the park two blocks away, put it in the rubbish bin, and went home, but I could *still* smell it.

I asked Lon if he wanted to eat it.

Lon ate it and then farted.

I could still smell it.

WHAT REGGIE DID ON THE WEEKEND 2

On the weekend I told everyone about this hilarious book I'd just finished called What Reggie Did on the Weekend. (Have you read it? Of course you have. You must have. You're right here on the last page.) Anyway, it was so good that I cried when it was finished. Okay, I might have made that up. The crying part, I mean. I didn't really cry. Instead, I followed Ma around the house and said "Please can I read book 2? Please can I read book 2? Please can I read book 2?" nine-hundred and twenty-one times. What's that? Yes, thank you, that is a remarkable achievement, isn't it? Yes, Ma's very proud of me.

Anyway, so now you're wondering if the second Reggie book is as good as the first Reggie book, right? Well, let's just say you may not own enough underpants to get through this one. Seriously.

www.LeeMWinter.com